STINGER
THE SEA PHANTOM

With special thanks to Michael Ford

For Bodhi Churchill

www.seaquestbooks.co.uk

ORCHARD BOOKS

First published in Great Britain in 2013 by Orchard Books
This edition published in 2016 by The Watts Publishing Group

5 7 9 10 8 6 4

Text © 2013 Beast Quest Limited.
Cover and inside illustrations by Artful Doodlers with special thanks to Bob and Justin
© Orchard Books 2013

Series created by Beast Quest Limited, London

A CIP catalogue record for this book is available from the British Library.

ISBN 978 1 40832 412 7

Printed in Great Britain by Clays Ltd, Elcograf S.p.A

The paper and board used in this book are made from wood from responsible sources

Orchard Books
An imprint of Hachette Children's Group
Part of The Watts Publishing Group Limited
Carmelite House, 50 Victoria Embankment, London EC4Y 0DZ

An Hachette UK Company
www.hachette.co.uk
www.hachettechildrens.co.uk

STINGER
THE SEA PHANTOM

BY ADAM BLADE

ORCHARD

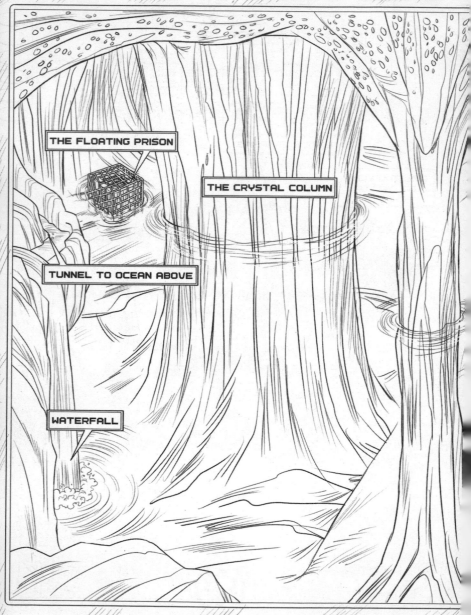

SPECTRON, 3,548 FATHOMS DEEP,
THE CAVERN OF GHOSTS

I've done it! At last I perfected my new invention. When the Professor strikes, I believe it could foil his evil plan…

Now I must find him. Someone has to stop him, and nobody knows him as well as I do. It will be hard to leave the Sea Ghosts unprotected. They are so kind and innocent, and have shared everything with me, all of their carefully collected treasures of the sea. I fear that they have even come to think of me as their guardian.

But I must leave if their world is to be saved. I can only hope that my new device will be enough to stop the Professor.

If it isn't, the Cavern of Ghosts – and everything that lies above – is doomed…

>LOG ENTRY ENDS

CHAPTER ONE

THE DEADLY RAINBOW

Max tinkered with his wrist-computer as he waited for Lia to catch up. A few little tweaks, and he would be able to use it as a remote control for his aquabuggy.

Spike streaked past, trailing bubbles, with Lia hunched close to the swordfish's back.

"Wait for me!" Max called. He gave up on the computer and pressed his foot down on the accelerator pedal. The aquabuggy plunged into Spike's wake. His dogbot

Rivet skimmed through the water at his side, leg propellers whizzing furiously. The ocean currents swirled through Max's hair and around his body. *This buggy is fast!* he thought.

Spike dipped his sword-nose and scooted across the seabed, coming to a sudden halt

beside what looked like a floating rock. Max pulled up alongside Lia and the swordfish. No, it wasn't a rock; it was a puffer-fish with grey, dappled skin. It drifted around, blown up like a balloon.

"Ball, Max!" Rivet barked. "Chase!"

The dogbot leaped forward. At once the puffer fish let all its air out and flashed away.

"Ball gone," barked Rivet, his tail drooping.

Lia shook her head. "You and your dogbot are still getting used to the undersea world, eh?" she asked.

Max grinned at her.

We call them Orb Fish, said a voice in his head.

Max had almost forgotten Ko was with them, sitting behind Lia with his arms clutched around her waist. The Sea Ghost boy's outline shimmered, his body as see-through as a bubble. Only his green glowing eyes were clearly visible.

"Please, Ko," Max said. "Less of the telepathy."

Sorry, Ko said, then, aloud: "I mean, sorry."

It was the Sea Ghost boy who'd led them here, to this vast underwater cavern beneath the ocean floor. The Cavern of Ghosts. It was a world not even Max's Merryn friend Lia had visited before. Her city, Sumara, lay directly above this mysterious place.

Lia, Ko and Max were all different species, but they shared the same enemy: Max's uncle, the Professor. Not content with trying to control the oceans above, he wanted to destroy the Cavern of Ghosts too. Max had already defeated one of the Professor's deadly Robobeasts. Shredder, a giant metal spider, had almost killed him with its stabbing hyperblade legs. Max dreaded to think what they'd have to face next. If the Professor succeeded in wiping out this world, Sumara, which lay directly above, would be destroyed too.

A groan beside Max made him turn. On the other seat of the buggy slumped Ko's poor mother, Allis. Like her son, her body was soft and see-through; it was hard to make out where her limbs ended and the sea began. But whereas her son's eyes were bright and glowing, hers had dimmed to a dull jade. She'd been held prisoner by the Professor in a floating prison, and had fallen ill.

Ko slid off Spike's back and swam to his mother's side with his strange pulsing rhythm. "Mother sickness worse," he said, stroking her head. "We must go to city quickly. Our healers help her."

"Of course," said Max. "Let's go."

Ko climbed back onto Spike, and Lia directed her swordfish into open waters. Max gunned the aquabuggy after her. He longed to give Spike a proper race, but he wasn't sure how Allis would cope with a bumpy ride.

As they skirted over the seabed, Max felt an ache in his heart. At least Ko had his mother back. Max hadn't seen his own mother since the day she'd set out on a voyage of discovery in her submarine, the *Leaping Dolphin*. Her co-pilot that day had been her brother, Max's uncle. But he'd turned on her. Rather than use their research for good, he'd wanted to steal the wealth and power of the underwater worlds. Now the Professor claimed to know where Max's mother was. Perhaps that was a lie, but Max had to keep searching until he found out the truth.

I sense you're grieving, said a weak female voice in his head.

Max turned to Allis. Waving locks of pale blue hair settled over her face, and a faint smile played on her lips. "I'm fine," he said. He could hardly tell her off for getting into his head like that. "How are you feeling?"

Hungry, said Allis.

Max speeded up a little until he was closer to the others. "We need to stop and eat," he called to his friends. Lia nodded.

They pulled up at the edge of a boulder field on the sea bed, and Lia drew out a couple of seaweed cakes from her knapsack. She handed one to Max.

Red kelp, he thought. *My favourite!*

When he'd first tasted Merryn food he'd wanted to spit it right back out, but not any more. It felt as though he was becoming more Merryn all the time. Part of him, though – the human part – still longed for the delicious cooking of his home city, Aquora, above the waves: meat pies, ripe fruit, salt candy...

He wondered what his dad was doing at

that very moment. His duties as the city's Chief Defence Engineer would keep him busy, of course, but was he thinking about Max? Or even about Max's mother?

Lia offered a cake to Ko, but the Sea Ghost held up a hand.

"What do your people eat then?" she asked.

Ko cocked his head. "Fish, of course."

With a deft turn, he swam off, quick as a darting eel. His body slid into a crack between two rocks.

"I thought you underwater folk didn't touch fish," Max said to Lia. "What about the three Rules of the Sea? Not harming other creatures…"

"That's Merryn Law," said Lia, with a frown. "Ghost people are different."

It wasn't long before Ko returned, a silver fish dangling from his mouth. He cradled his mother's head, and started feeding it to her.

Rivet nudged Max with his nose, eyes bright. "Rivet hunt too?" he barked.

"Certainly not!" said Lia, crossing her arms.

"Sorry, Rivet," said Max, patting his dogbot on the head. He tucked into his seaweed cake, sitting astride his buggy seat with the others gathered close. Everyone was being friendly enough, but Max knew Lia still didn't trust the Sea Ghosts. After all, Ko had betrayed them to the Professor once before. He'd had good reason, with his mother held captive, but still...

Rivet began to bark, eyes flashing.

"Hey," Max said. "Lia already told you – no hunting."

"No, Max," barked Rivet. "Noise."

Then Max heard it too – a buzzing through the water, like an approaching swarm of bees.

He peered about him as the sound grew

louder. Then, off to his left, he saw a school of hundreds of tiny white fish swimming towards them, like a blizzard moving through the water. In a blink of an eye, the shoal changed direction, becoming red, then purple, then blue.

"They're beautiful!" said Lia.

The school engulfed them in a cloud of dazzling colour. Rivet's head jerked back and forth as he tried to follow their movements. Max reached out, and watched the shoal break around his hand.

"We name them Deadly Rainbow," said Ko.

"Ouch!" said Max as a shock jolted his wrist. "They're electric!"

Rivet whimpered and huddled closer to Max.

"One shock no harm," said Ko, "but many is death. Deadly Rainbow friend. Most times."

"Most of the time?" said Lia nervously. Max had never seen her so anxious – the Merryn prided themselves on knowing everything about the underwater world.

Ko placed his hand gently into the shoal. *They normally only attack when threatened,* he said silently. *We Sea Ghosts say they can sense a good heart.*

The rainbow fish left them, buzzing and crackling.

Max stared after them, open-mouthed. He wondered if his mother ever came across the Deadly Rainbow fish – she loved nothing more than investigating new species. And they wouldn't have hurt her. Would they? "Let's follow them," he said.

"We need to take Allis to the Sea Ghost City," said Lia.

"We'll only be a few minutes," said Max. "And you heard what Ko said: they're not really dangerous."

I'll be fine, said Ko's mother.

Lia didn't look convinced.

"Come on," said Max. "We need a bit of

fun after battling Shredder. Don't tell me you aren't even a tiny bit excited!"

"Oh, all right," said Lia, climbing back onto Spike.

Max grabbed Rivet's collar to hitch a ride, and the dogbot yapped excitedly. "Follow the Deadly Rainbow fish!" Max shouted.

Rivet's leg propellers whined and he shot after the shoal, dragging Max along with him.

Be careful... came Ko's voice.

CHAPTER TWO

JOLLY ROGER'S RETURN

Soon they'd left the aquabuggy far behind. Water streamed through Max's clothes as Rivet shot through the currents.

The Deadly Rainbow shoal was fast. It suddenly dipped out of sight over a rocky ledge, thinning and flowing like a sparkling waterfall. Max grinned.

"After them, Riv!" he said.

The dogbot angled his body into a dive to follow, but Lia caught Max's trailing leg.

"Wait!" she said. "Can't you hear that?"

Max let go of Rivet, who swam in a circle, chasing his own tail and growling. "Shush, boy," he said.

As Rivet powered down, Max heard a human wail over the buzzing of the Deadly Rainbow. "Ah…oh… Aargh! Get off me!"

Someone's in trouble! Max scanned the rocks below, then pointed to where the fish were gathered around a large patch of seaweed. "It's coming from down there!"

They swam cautiously towards the shoal.

Beneath the rocky ledge, a figure wearing a deepsuit was huddled in a ball. The fish darted around him, delivering their tiny shocks. The stranger's cries fizzed and crackled through his helmet's microphone.

"Ouch…eek…shiver-me-tim— Ooh!"

I know that voice… thought Max.

Through the shifting cloud of fish, Max

made out a thin face with an eye patch. The man's long hair was tied back in a ponytail.

"Roger!" said Lia and Max at the same time.

The pirate had been another of the Professor's captives, held in Shredder's web-like prison. Max and Lia had helped him escape, but he'd left them with barely a word of thanks or farewell. Now he was jerking this way and that as the Deadly Rainbow tormented him, sparks flying as they brushed past him.

"We have to get him out of there!" said Max, kicking off towards Roger.

Lia tugged him back. "Careful, Max!" she said. "Remember what Ko said. Too many shocks can kill a person."

Roger hadn't spotted them. He was writhing and swatting, and with each cry the Deadly Rainbow only seemed to get angrier. His gold tooth flashed as he squirmed.

Rivet chewed Max's sleeve with his teeth. "Max, look!" he said.

Max flipped over in the water and faced the way his dogbot's snout was pointing. On the far side of the rocky outcrop, a grey shape lay on the seabed. At first Max thought it might be a big dead fish, but as his eyes focused he saw it was just an old-fashioned rubber dinghy, with rotting wooden oars still dangling from its sides like flopping arms. Max had seen boats like that in history books back in the Aquora City Library.

"It must have been down here for hundreds of years," he said.

"So what use is that?" said Lia.

Rivet shot off at top speed, and scooped up both oars in his teeth.

"Of course!" Max said. He remembered how he'd used a Merryn pearl spear against Silda the Electric Eel... "Clever boy." He took one of the oars and handed the other to Lia. "We can't touch the Deadly Rainbow, but the wood won't conduct their electricity."

"That's good thinking for a dog," said Lia.

"Seems to me he's adjusting to the undersea world just fine," said Max.

Roger's thrashing had reached fever pitch.

"No…eeee…aargh… Holy calamari!"

Holding the oars at arm's length, Max and
Lia plunged them into the dancing, zapping
fish. The shoal split apart, leaving a narrow
gap in between the two oars. Roger's eyes lit
up behind his visor when he saw them. He
pressed a button on his wrist, and his boot-
thrusters sent him powering upwards out of
harm's way.

Almost at once, the Deadly Rainbow shoal
seemed to lose interest, and darted off.

Roger shuddered and Max noticed that his ponytail had come loose. A few of his hairs were standing on end. "So, you again," he said.

"And perhaps a little thank you for rescuing you?" said Lia, with her hands on her hips. Roger's hands trembled as he tucked his stray locks away.

"Rescuing me?" he said. "You, er... you found me right in the middle of some scientific research, actually. I was studying that new species of colourful fish." He cast a worried glance after the departing shoal.

"Studying?" said Max. With the ponytail, eye patch and gold tooth, Roger didn't look much like a scientist.

"Indeed," said the pirate. "They became a bit upset. I'll be all right in a brace of shakes... I mean, in a few minutes."

"They're called the Deadly Rainbow," said

Lia. "And with good reason. Our Sea Ghost friend told us to steer clear."

Roger looked around them. "Looks like you sent him packing at last," he said. "And not a moment too soon. Useless crew, those Sea Ghosts. Nothing but trouble."

"I heard that!" said a voice that made all three of them turn.

Ko was hovering above the rocky ledge. The soft features of his face were set in a scowl and his green eyes narrowed. "I'd have left you to the Deadly Rainbow," he said. He jerked a thumb over his shoulder. "We go now. Mother ill."

"No need to sulk," said Roger, with an elaborate bow towards Ko. "No harm meant, my transparent friend."

Max felt a stab of guilt. *I should never have suggested this little adventure. We should be heading to Spectron, in case the Professor strikes there next.*

"Well, we'll leave you to your research," said Lia, her lips curling into a smile. "We're heading to Ko's home now."

"Spectron?" said Roger. "The Ghost City?"

"Ko's mother has a fever," said Max. "She needs medicine." He gripped Rivet's collar again. "Let's go, Riv."

"Wait!" called Roger. "Don't leave me... I mean, I'm heading to Spectron too." He lowered his voice to a whisper. "To be honest, shipmates, you'll need someone to protect you in that place. It's a den of thieves."

Lia rolled her eyes at Max, who grinned.

"Follow us, then," he said. "It might be handy having a pira— I mean, a scientist...in our gang in case the Professor attacks again."

Roger grinned back, and his gold tooth twinkled. "Right you are! Plot a course for the City of Ghosts!"

CHAPTER THREE

CITY OF THE SEA GHOSTS

Back at the aquabuggy, Ko's mother was sitting up straighter, and some life seemed to have returned to her eyes. "How are you feeling?" asked Max.

"Better," she said. "Spectron not far now."

She struggled to get up but slumped back. *She's just putting on a brave face*, thought Max.

"Quite a ragtag crew you've gathered," said Roger. "You'll be needing a captain."

"And let me guess," said Lia. "You'd be willing?"

"If I must," said Roger with a grin. Max rolled his eyes.

They set off together, Max and Allis on the buggy, Lia on Spike, and Ko leading the way. Roger powered beside them with his thruster boots, Rivet snapping playfully at his heels. The pirate didn't seem to be enjoying it much. "Get this scurvy cur away from me, will you?"

Max laughed. "Leave him alone, Riv."

The dogbot didn't seem to hear, and wagged his tail faster. With a burst of speed from his thrusters, Roger left Rivet trailing.

The ocean floor sloped downwards. They travelled between strange smooth boulders covered with patches of sea moss. There were no fish down here, which gave the whole place an eerie feeling, like an underwater desert.

The water darkened and the temperature cooled. Max noticed that Allis had dropped into a doze.

Lia guided Spike up alongside Max's buggy, and glanced at the sleeping Sea Ghost. "Are you sure we're doing the right thing?" she whispered.

"What do you mean?" asked Max.

"Well, can we trust them – the Sea Ghosts?"

Ko was still swimming at the front, effortlessly rippling his body through the water.

"I think so," said Max. Then, more firmly, "Anyway, we can't just leave Allis."

Lia nodded with pursed lips and drifted away. But she'd planted a seed of doubt in Max's mind. *Ko wouldn't betray us again, surely...*

At that moment they reached the edge of a ridge. Max gasped when he saw what lay below. Allis stirred beside him.

Welcome to Spectron, she said in his head.

At first it looked like a dumping ground. Hundreds of buildings of all shapes and sizes were scattered at the bottom of the canyon. Some were metal, others made of vegetation. Rusting walls butted up against roofs of seaweed. Narrow streets threaded in between. It was nothing like Aquora, where the city was laid out in a perfect grid between

the looming skyscrapers. Or like Sumara, a city made entirely of glowing weeds and coral.

"Wait a moment!" Max said. "Those aren't buildings...they're—"

"Ships," Lia finished for him. "Or the remains of them."

As his eyes swept over the city, Max made out propellers, masts and keels, jutting out of the buildings. Portholes of all shapes and

sizes pocked the structures. His gaze fell on decks and landing winches, spars and rigging, some modern and some ancient.

"It's a wreck yard," said Roger.

"You rude man," said Ko.

The largest vessel was the complete hull of an Aquoran battleship from some forgotten war centuries before. Judging by the great tear along its flank, Max guessed it must have been sunk by a torpedo. But there were hundreds...no, thousands...of other vessels. Fishing boats, cruise vessels, cargo ships, pleasure yachts, hovercraft, tugboats, landing craft, speedboats... All sunk and wrecked on the seabed.

"We use what we find," said Ko.

"Scavengers," muttered Roger.

"You really should learn some manners," said Max.

"He right," said Allis quietly. "Sea Ghosts

not build. Sea Ghosts collect and use."

"Not waste," added Ko.

As they descended towards the city, Max hardly knew which way to look. Everywhere, recycled bits of ships and machinery had been put to use. He saw what looked like an aquabike's headlamp used to light the street. The loading hatch of a cargo ship was a front door to a house, weighed closed with an anchor and chain. Two Sea Ghost children were playing frisbee with a ship's wheel.

"Play fetch!" barked Rivet.

"Not now, Riv," said Max.

The Sea Ghosts slid off through an open porthole, their bodies warping to fit through the gap. Roger sidled up beside Max. "I'd bet my one good eye they've got some treasure down here too," he muttered, casting a glance at Ko.

"I'm sure they have," said Max, "but as a scientist, you wouldn't be interested in that, I suppose?"

"Only in items of historical interest," said Roger quickly.

The city was strangely quiet, apart from the soft thrum of the aquabuggy's engines and Allis's coughs. Max thought he saw a movement up on the deck of an old catamaran, but when he looked again there was nothing there. Every so often, he thought he saw a face at a window, but they quickly vanished.

"Where is everyone?" asked Lia.

"They here," said Ko. "Ghost people shy. Strangers not in Spectron many times."

A bell began to toll slowly, echoing through the water. Then suddenly a Sea Ghost appeared over the gunwale of a fishing boat and shot towards them at top speed. Max felt Roger grab his shoulders and land behind him on

the buggy. The pirate pointed his blaster pistol over Max's shoulder.

"Stay back, Ghost!" he called.

The Sea Ghost paused, his body only a faint outline in the water.

"I mean no harm," he said.

"Then let's see your hands," said Roger.

The Sea Ghost shrugged and held them out for Roger to inspect.

"Put the gun away," said Max, pushing Roger off the buggy. "He's obviously not armed."

"Can't be too careful," said the pirate. "Turn your back, and one of these lousy Ghosts'll put a knife in it."

One by one, Max became aware of other Sea Ghost people all around, peeping over decks, from behind masts, and through portholes. Hundreds of pairs of glowing green eyes watched them. Had they been there all along?

"They're scared, you fool!" said Lia, slipping off Spike's back and swimming across to Roger. She grabbed his arm and tried to wrestle the pistol away. Roger struggled back, and a shot sizzled harmlessly into a steel hull. The green eyes shrank away as one.

"Be careful!" said Max. But he was pleased Lia was sticking up for the Sea Ghosts at last.

"Let go!" said Roger. "I'm only trying to—"
In a flash, Rivet darted beneath their arms and

snapped the pistol out of Roger's hand with his teeth. "Oh, perfect," said Roger. "We'll be keel-hauled before you can say 'cat-o-nine-tails'!"

Seeing the pistol out of the pirate's hand and safely in Rivet's jaws, the Sea Ghosts began slowly to emerge from their hiding

places. Like hundreds of jellyfish, they pulsed down to gather around Max and his friends. Allis moaned softly from the aquabuggy, and Ko swam to his mother's side.

Though Max couldn't hear Ko or his mother speaking, he saw the Sea Ghosts turning to each other and nodding. The Ghost man who'd first approached them swam forward.

"Welcome to our city," he said out loud, bowing slightly.

"Mother needs medicine," said Ko, taking one of her arms. "Help me take her to the healer."

Lia let go of Roger and swam over to help Ko. Together, the two of them set off with Allis supported between them.

Roger winked at Max. "I don't know about you, but I've got some plundering – I mean, some *exploring* to do. See you later!"

He engaged his boot-thrusters and shot away down a passage.

I can't let him go off on his own, Max thought. But the aquabuggy wouldn't fit down the narrow track. "Rivet, here!"

His dogbot shot over, and Max stowed the pistol in the compartment built into his back. "Sorry about this," he said to the Sea Ghosts, gripping the dogbot's collar. "Catch the pirate, boy!"

Rivet tore down the alley after Roger, with Max hanging onto his dogbot as tightly as he could. From the rows of cabins on either side, Max realised it was actually the corridor of an old cruise ship.

"Roger could be anywhere!" he said. "Sniff him out, Riv!"

Rivet's powerful nasal sensors could detect different species of fish at half a mile, so finding one smelly pirate wouldn't be a problem. They burst out at the far end of the passage and the battleship up loomed before them. Max guessed it was the council chamber, where the elders of Spectron met. But there was no sign of Roger.

Rivet's nose tilted left and right, and Max's eyes swept over the landscape of abandoned ships. He did a double take, and his breath caught in his throat. It couldn't be...

One of the buildings alongside the great battleship was a submarine, sleek but strongly built, and much newer than the surrounding buildings. It didn't look much different from the other salvaged vessels, apart from one thing – the symbol painted on its hull.

A great silvery dolphin, jumping proudly from the waves.

Max swallowed. His skin tingled.

The *Leaping Dolphin*.

His mother's ship.

CHAPTER FOUR

PAINFUL MEMORIES

"This way, Max!" barked Rivet, tugging off to the left. "Bad pirate man!"

Max let go of his dogbot's collar. "Not now, Riv," he said quietly. "This is more important."

He paddled down towards the sub, feeling oddly hot inside. He hadn't seen the vessel since the day he'd waved goodbye to his mother at Aquora's harbour, all those years ago. And even then, he had only the vaguest

memory of a beautiful woman waving
goodbye and then disappearing into the
sub. Mostly, he remembered missing her
afterwards.

His father told him that most other
people in Aquora had thought Max's mum
and her brother were mad. He'd shown

Max the story that the city's holopaper had carried in a tiny column:

CRACKPOT EXPLORERS GO FISHING FOR MERRYN.

No one had believed in the Merryn then. They still didn't, in fact. But his mum had been right all along – Max knew that now.

Rivet floated slowly to his side. "Old ship, Max," he said, cocking his head. "Pirate man other way."

"Not just any old ship, boy," Max replied. He'd built Riv after the disappearance, so the dogbot didn't recognise the *Leaping Dolphin*.

Max ran his fingers over the banged-up hull, then cast a sad glance around the debris of the Sea Ghost city. "You were here, weren't you, Mum?" he murmured.

What's "mum"? came a voice.

Max turned around and saw a whole

crowd of Sea Ghosts swarming towards him. Suddenly a dozen different voices hit him like waves:

Weird clothes...

...fish or boy...

...trust him?...

...friend of Ko...

The Sea Ghosts pulled at his hair and clothes. Max put his hands over his ears but it did nothing to stop the sounds inside his head.

What material...?

...who are you...?

...where are you from...?

"Please!" he said. "One at a time."

One of the Sea Ghosts pushed the others back. Max guessed she was a girl from the delicate outline of her features.

Are you a Merryn? she asked.

"No," Max said. "I'm a Breather... I mean,

a human. From above the waves. But I was given the Merryn Touch, so I can breathe underwater and speak their language."

Why are you here?

Max frowned. Ko had said the Sea Ghosts knew all about him. Had that been a lie too, just to flatter him and draw him here? "Ko brought us," Max said. "He said you needed our help."

Your help with what? echoed back from several minds.

Max felt his frustration building. "To face the Professor, of course. The man with the giant machines. He wants to control all creatures under the sea."

He thought about those he'd already defeated: Cephalox the Cyber Squid, Silda the Electric Eel, Manak the Silent Predator and Kraya the Blood Shark, not to mention Shredder the Spider Droid. He wondered what the next enemy would look like, and when it would strike. Perhaps the Sea Ghosts could read the scary images in his mind, because they shrank back as one, their eyes widening in fear.

"But listen," said Max, putting his hand to the hatch of the *Leaping Dolphin*, "I have to know, did any of you meet the woman who came in this submarine?"

The Sea Ghosts muttered to each other. Max picked up words like "woman", and "saviour", and even, "Don't tell him."

"Don't tell me what?" he asked.

The Sea Ghosts parted and one pulsed his way to the front. He looked older than the others, with a flowing white beard like tendrils of transparent seaweed. He held a metal key, which he slotted into the door. With a creak, he pulled it open.

Instead of an airlock, inside was a porch

hung with glowing lanterns.

"Come into my home," said the old Sea Ghost, aloud. He spoke much better Merryn than Ko.

"Your home?" said Max. "But... Wait here, Riv." Rivet cocked his head, eyes flashing. "Don't worry – I won't be long."

With his heart in his mouth, Max followed the old Sea Ghost through the hatch. As soon as he saw the interior, his heart sank. The inside of the sub was filled with furniture made from scrap metal, and the walls were decorated with seaweed and shells. Clearly none of this was his mum's. Max felt a rush of anger. What had this Sea Ghost done to his mother's ship?

"I did meet the human woman you speak of," said the Sea Ghost, settling into a chair. "She taught me her language. For a time, she was our guardian here. She tried to

protect us against the evil man with his
monsters."

"Tried?" said Max, fearing the worst.

"She left Spectron to face him," said the
Sea Ghost. "She thought that somehow she
could persuade him to be good."

Of course she did, thought Max. *She was his sister...*

"And?"

The Sea Ghost lowered his eyes. "And she never returned. We have faith that she will, one day – when we need her the most."

Max swallowed back his grief. *Then we've got something in common.*

"I sense your concern," the Sea Ghost said. "But she gave this vessel to me as a home, I swear it."

Max cast his eyes over the room. He had no doubt the Sea Ghost was telling the truth. There were hints of his mother all over the sea. Would he be chasing these half-clues forever?

In the corner of the room, something caught Max's eye, and he swam over. On a lampstand made from carved coral lay a conch shell he thought he recognised. His dad had one just like it in their apartment back in Aquora.

"Where did you get this?" he asked.

The Sea Ghost smiled. "That's the only one of her possessions I have left," he said. "I've no idea what it's for."

Max picked it up, and was surprised to see it was no ordinary shell. On the underside, someone had attached some complex robotics. Fine wires twisted over a circuit board, spiralling into the depths of the shell. *Did my mother make this?* Max wondered.

"It's funny," said the old Sea Ghost. "The woman – she looked a bit like you."

Max replaced the shell. "That's because she was...she is...my moth—"

A great grinding sound drowned out his words, and the vessel shook like it was in the grip of an earthquake. The shell fell off the table and Max caught it, steadying himself against the wall.

"What in all the Seven Seas of Nemos was that?" said Max.

CHAPTER FIVE

A MONSTER AWAKES

Max replaced the shell and swam quickly to the door. Rivet was waiting outside, his tail between his legs.

"It's okay, boy," said Max.

He saw Spike shooting up another street towards him with Lia on his back. Her eyes were wide with alarm.

"I thought I'd never find you," she said. "Did you feel that?"

"I certainly did," said Max. "Where are Ko

and Allis? Are they safe?"

"I left them with the healer," said Lia. "Allis is going to be fine. Where's Roger?"

"I lost him."

Another rumble shook the city, weaker than the first. All the buildings shifted slightly. Max noticed several Sea Ghosts still gathered nearby, but they didn't seem bothered by the strange shaking.

"Hey," Max called over. "What's going on?"

A small Sea Ghost girl drifted over, her outline rosy. *Must be the Sea Ghost version of a blush*, thought Max.

"Nothing to fear," she said softly. "It has bad dream."

"'It'?" said Max and Lia together.

But the girl was already swimming away with the strange pulsing motion, to hide shyly behind the keel of a wrecked vessel.

"Maybe we should talk to Ko about this," said Max.

Lia nodded, then glanced around her. "Hold on – where's Spike?"

Max caught sight of the swordfish below them on the seabed, tailfins pointed up as he nosed at something on the ground. He swished his sword at Lia.

"He's found something," she said, swimming down.

Max followed, with Rivet at his side. Lia landed on the ocean floor and pushed aside handfuls of seaweed and pebbles. "What do we make of this?" she asked.

Max inspected the ground. It looked like grey rock. "I think they call it 'rock.'"

Lia stared at him icily. "Take a closer look, Breather boy."

Max moved his face closer and reached out. As soon as he touched the seabed, he jerked his hand back. "It's warm!" He ran his fingers across it. It wasn't rock at all. It was smooth and slightly soft. "It feels like…"

"Skin!" said Lia.

Max swallowed. It reminded him of the leathery hide of Manak, the Silent Predator. They had landed on one of his great wings, thinking it was the sea floor. But in fact, they were standing on one of the Professor's Robobeasts.

Max kicked off the seabed and gave his wrist transmitter a twist. A few seconds later, the aquabuggy skirted over the top of a nearby building and drifted towards them.

"It works!" said Max, taking out the first aid kit.

"What do you need that for?" Lia asked. "Is someone hurt?"

"No," said Max, "but I have a theory and I want to test it."

He found a stethoscope in the case, and inserted the earpieces. Then he touched the chestpiece to the silver-grey seabed. At first there was only eerie silence, then a soft boom. Silence, then another boom. The rhythm settled into a regular pattern. *A heartbeat.*

"I think we've found what 'it' is," he said.

He unhooked one of the earpieces and placed it to Lia's ear. Her eyes went wide.

"It's a creature," she said. "Spectron must be built on top of it!"

"And it must be huge!" said Max.

The ground shook again, and a blast of sound tore through Max's ears. He snatched the wires away. "It doesn't sound happy," he said. "I don't think it's just a bad dream."

He looked about him, and saw that all the Sea Ghosts had fled.

"I wish they weren't so nervous," said Lia, looking pretty nervous herself.

Another jolt of sound – this time a high-pitched screaming – assaulted Max's ears. But now it wasn't through the stethoscope, it was deep inside his head.

He pressed his hands to his ears, but it was no use. The wailing continued in anguished waves, and a hundred voices called out the same word:

Help!

"The Sea Ghosts!" Max said. "Come on!"

He jumped into the aquabuggy's seat and took the controls. The buggy jolted as it began to climb through the water, above most of the buildings of Spectron. Max scanned the ground, looking for any Sea Ghosts in trouble. But he couldn't see any sign of the creature emerging from the sea floor.

"No, Max!" said Lia. "Look up!"

He stared into the distance, and his breath lodged in his throat. A creature rose up behind the massive battleship, even bigger than the Sea Ghosts' council chambers. Or was it a creature? It looked like a cloud of heaving, pink, semi-transparent slime. Within its jelly-like body, Max made out red branches of veins and organs, but all arranged in perfect rows and columns.

Just like a giant circuit board, he thought.

"Big jellyfish, Max," said Rivet.

Max nodded, and reached out to stroke Rivet's head reassuringly.

Pink stinger tendrils dangled menacingly from the creature, each one twisting and swirling in the sea currents, searching for prey. They ended in cruel-looking barbs of twisted metal that sent out sparks of electricity. Like a drifting cloud, the monster loomed stealthily through the water. As it approached the buildings of Spectron it lashed out with its tendrils, destroying one after another of the Sea Ghosts' homes. Max could hear more cries for help.

We've got to stop it! he thought.

"That's not a living creature," said Lia. Max turned and saw his friend hovering in the water with Spike. "Only one person could have created something like that."

"The Professor," Max breathed.

CHAPTER SIX

STINGER'S RETURN

In the blink of an eye, Max was surrounded by Sea Ghosts. Their outlines flickered darkly as they bundled him off the aquabuggy. *Can't stay here*, said a voice.

"Hey, wait!" said Max, struggling to free himself. He saw Lia and her swordfish swept along too. It was like being in the grip of a powerful current. Rivet growled as he was pushed through the water. Spike, swimming furiously, managed to slip free, and darted

back and forth around the group.

Not safe, said another voice. *Must flee...*

"We have to stay and fight!" said Max. "The Professor must be stopped. We can't leave your home."

We must take cover, said the voice. Max and his friends were carried to shelter beneath an upturned vessel – a hull of rusted steel, propped up at one end. An old searchlight lit the enclosed space, picking out the outlines of several dozen cowering Sea Ghosts. Spike slid under the rim of the hull and joined them, waving his nose-sword in excitement. Max wondered where Roger had got to. If he was out there, he was in terrible danger.

"Listen to us," said the old Sea Ghost from the *Leaping Dolphin*. He swam in front of Max and Lia. "When Stinger the Sea Phantom comes, we flee. It's our way."

"But…wait," said Lia. "You mean that thing has come before?"

The old Sea Ghost nodded. *Many times. We know when it is coming because Spectron shakes.*

"There's something – a creature – beneath the city, isn't there?" said Lia.

The Sea Ghosts looked at her and then at each other, but said nothing.

Max knelt down to peer under the hull's rim. The giant jellyfish was floating ever closer, its tentacles reaching into cracks between the city's buildings.

"We try to fight Stinger before," said the Sea Ghost, "but we lose many." He sighed. "The Phantom shows no mercy."

Another Sea Ghost, an old woman, approached them. *It's taken years to collect all these wrecks and build our beautiful city. If we run away, Stinger gives up and leaves Spectron in peace.*

The fear in the woman's eyes made Max angry. "But you can't run away forever," he said. "We need to show the Professor that he can't boss people around."

"You can't live your lives in fear," Lia added.

The Sea Ghosts all looked at them sadly. *Why not?* they said as one.

Max's was frustrated. Though it wasn't his

fault, he couldn't help feeling responsible that a Breather, one of his own kind, was terrorising the innocent species of the ocean.

"Listen to me," he said. "We know who's behind this Stinger. We've faced him before, and beaten him. The time for running away is over."

The Sea Ghosts didn't speak for some time, but Max could feel their doubts and fears washing over him.

"The nice woman from above said the same thing," said the old Sea Ghost. "She said she would go to our enemy and fix things."

But she never came back, said the female Sea Ghost.

The old man looked at her. *She might return...*

No – she abandoned us.

Max gritted his teeth. He tried not to think about his mother and what might have happened to her. Whatever it was, she must have failed, because the Professor's creature was here now, pressing down on them.

"That woman was my mother," Max said. The Sea Ghosts gasped. "Just as you once trusted her, I ask you to trust me. If you won't fight yourselves, let me and Lia fight for you."

The old man smiled. "I thought that you looked a bit like her." *Perhaps we should do as the boy says*, he added silently.

The other Sea Ghosts looked at each other. Their voices were too confused for Max to follow properly, but he felt their doubts weighing heavy in the water.

Too dangerous...

...just a boy...

...Stinger will be angry...

"If we don't destroy the creature," said Lia, "it will keep coming back. And when it's finished with Spectron, what's to stop it attacking other cities?"

I trust them, said the old man over the other voices. *Maybe this boy is destined to help us. He followed his mother here, after all.*

A few of the Sea Ghosts swam to Max's side, while others remained stubbornly where they were. Max didn't blame them. He wasn't even sure what he could do to stop the Professor's evil creature. *I hope I'm not leading them to their deaths*, he thought.

The old man faced him. "We will join you," he said.

Max peered out, and saw the jellyfish's shallow falling over their hiding place. He felt like a sardine before a shark. Stinger's tendrils unfolded like great vines from a tree.

"Let's go!" Max said.

As Max left the shelter of the hull, Rivet nudged him with his metal snout. "Stay, Max!" he barked.

"Not this time," said Max. "We've got to fight."

Rivet whined, but followed him. As they emerged into open water, they heard a crash from a nearby submarine-house. "Come on, you little beauty," said a familiar voice. Roger stumbled out of the door, a great golden platter clutched to his chest. When he saw Max and Lia, he grinned sheepishly. "Oh, I was just looking for you two," he said.

"Hmm." Lia raised an eyebrow. "What do you think you're doing?"

"Stealing, by the looks of it," said Max.

Roger dropped the platter and shrugged. "Don't know what you're talking about," he said. A silver cup fell out of his pocket. "Ah."

"Typical pirate," said Max.

Roger shook his head. "For the last time, I'm not a..." He tipped his head back, noticing the enormous jellyfish. "Shiver me timbers

and blister me barnacles!" cried Roger. "What in all the seven seas is that?"

Max gritted his teeth. "That's one of the Professor's Robobeasts," he said. "And *you're* going to help us defeat it!"

CHAPTER SEVEN

FIGHTING THE SLIME

The Sea Phantom's tendrils trailed over the top of the huge battleship at the heart of Spectron. They left a coating of slime that oozed down the side of the hull. Max marvelled at the complex machinery he could see inside the creature's body – wheels, levers and hydraulics moving in perfect harmony. The goo that surrounded it must be to keep the mechanics protected from the water, Max realised.

It had taken a brilliant mind to construct such a robot. Brilliant and evil.

"If we're going to stop that thing, we need to disable its computer," Max said. "That means getting through the slime."

Lia frowned. "I had a feeling you were going to say that."

Max turned to the few brave Sea Ghosts who'd joined them. "Fetch spears," he said. "We need to pierce Stinger's body."

The old Sea Ghost frowned. "People of Spectron don't use weapons," he said. "We're peaceful."

"Well, fetch long pointy things then," said Lia. "It's time to fight."

Like a shoal bursting apart, the Sea Ghosts darted in several directions at once. Stinger had lifted up a giant cruiser in one of its tendrils. It held the vessel in front of what must have been its face. Two video cameras, mounted on hydraulic arms, swivelled around the cruiser's hull. *It's looking for something,* thought Max. The Sea Phantom dropped the

ship like a child bored with a toy. The cruiser crushed another ship-house flat and threw up a cloud of sand.

So much for leaving the city alone. Ko was right to lead us here.

Max snatched his hyperblade from the aquabuggy and climbed into the seat. Rivet clamped his paws onto the back.

"Ready?" Max called to Lia.

She was jumping onto Spike's back. "Ready," she said. "Let's show the Professor what we're made of!"

The Sea Ghosts were starting to reappear, all clutching sections of marine debris – spars, sharpened timbers, old metal antennae and even a fishing rod. *Hardly an army*, Max

thought, *but it's all we've got*. He noticed Roger had vanished again. "What a surprise..." he muttered.

Max gunned the buggy's nose up beneath Stinger's jiggling belly. Fronds of slimy skin waved gently in the water, but even in those flapping skirts of flesh, Max could see delicate wiring. Electricity sparked and flashed as the Sea Phantom moved.

Lia shot past him. "Max, look there!" she said, pointing into the very depths of the Professor's creation. "See that cylinder, right in the middle."

Max saw it at once. Among all the moving parts was a tube that seemed filled with swirling light. "It must be the control hub," he said.

"Stinger's brain," muttered Lia.

Max steered the buggy in an arc, flashing past the Sea Ghost forces. "Aim for that bright cylinder," he said. "Pierce it if you can!"

As he pointed the buggy towards the monster, he wielded his hyperblade.

"For Spectron!" he yelled. The Sea Ghosts streamed past him, brandishing scavenged weapons. Max saw them plunge their spears into Stinger's flesh, but the tips became stuck in the ooze. It was thicker than it looked.

The Sea Phantom jolted and jerked in the water, and sparks flashed across its body like lightning in the clouds. A noise like the roar of a distant waterfall filled the ocean.

We've made him angry, thought Max.

He leapt off the aquabuggy and lunged with his hyperblade. It sank into the slime and became lodged. Max tore it free and hacked again but with no luck. Further along the Sea Phantom's body, Lia was directing Spike to stab at the jellyfish's membrane with his nose-sword. The swordfish drove into the creature's flesh over and over again.

"It's too tough!" Lia called, then: "Look out!"

Max turned and saw a robotic limb looping through the water towards him, with a deadly metal spike attached. He jerked back and it missed him by a fraction. All across Stinger's body, limbs wriggled into life, tingling to find prey. The Sea Ghosts swam between the dangling tentacles, stabbing and slicing with their spears. Rivet snapped at one, clamping his jaws over it. Stinger thrashed and hurled the dogbot loose. Max dodged another tendril and hacked again.

A piercing scream echoed in Max's head, and he saw a Sea Ghost twitching in the vine-like grip of Stinger. The tendril coiled around the Sea Ghost's waist and the barbed tip touched his neck. A crackle of

light sparked across his body and he fell limp, limbs sagging.

That's why they call him Stinger, Max realised, hoping the Robobeast's victim would wake up.

No! Ambryn! shouted a voice. *Brother!*

Another Sea Ghost shot to the rescue of the first, sliding in and out of the reaching tentacles. He didn't see the one snaking towards him from behind until too late. The tendril snatched at his ankle and lifted him towards the jellied body. Max watched in horror as Stinger pushed the Sea Ghost into the sticky slime. Soon he was entirely encased inside a gooey prison.

One by one, the Sea Ghosts threw themselves at the Professor's creature, and each time it batted them away with shocks or snatched them up into its body. Soon a dozen of the poor people of Spectron were caught, dangling helplessly from Stinger's tendrils.

Max felt dread grip him by the throat. *It's all my fault. We can't fight the Robobeast like this. With all those stinging tentacles, it's more than a match for us.*

A tendril almost caught him, but Max rolled out of the way. He watched one of the Sea Ghosts struggling in the grip of the slime like a fly on a spider's web. And suddenly, he had a plan. They couldn't defeat this Beast through force alone. *We have to be clever.*

He needed to get close, and the only way to do that was if Stinger didn't see him as a threat...

Max jerked hard right to avoid a tendril. He steered the buggy upwards and arrived at Lia's side.

"I'm going to play dead," he told her. "Make myself easy prey."

"You must be mad!" she said. "What if it snatches you and traps you in its slime?"

"If I can get inside Stinger," Max said, "I'll be closer to its brain."

"Or maybe you'll end up dead!" said Lia.

Max stared at the nasty creature, which was drifting slowly on the current like a deadly cloud.

"Scared, Max," said Rivet.

"I'm scared too," he said. "But if I don't at least try we might all die, and Stinger will tear the city to pieces."

Lia's face was pinched. "Just be careful," she told him.

Max patted Rivet on the head, and tucked his hyperblade in his belt. "Stay here, boy." Rivet whined as Max shot off on the aquabuggy, directly into the path of Stinger. He killed the engines and slid off the seat, letting the buggy shoot ahead. He could pick it up later.

If there was a later.

Max let his body flop in the water like a dead fish. He closed his eyes to slits, and tried to still his thumping heart. Stinger loomed towards him, a silent stalking menace.

Come and get me, thought Max.

CHAPTER EIGHT

IN THE GRIP OF TERROR

Through his half-closed eyes, Max spied a tendril snaking through the water towards him, trailing slime. He could see tiny hooks along the edges. At first the touch was soft as it looped across his chest.

Then it gripped him and slime began to ooze over his body.

Max sucked in a deep breath as Stinger picked him up and stuffed him into its pink body. The goo closed over him like a wet,

clenching fist. Panic gripped Max's chest as slime clogged his gills. It seemed to be all around him, and his arms felt heavy. He began to struggle, trying to reach for the hyperblade, but he could hardly move. The pressure built under his temples and black spots pricked behind his eyes.

Lia was right, he thought. *This was a big*

mistake. I'm going to fail, just like my mother before me.

An image of her face flashed up before his eyes – smiling and waving goodbye as she stepped into the *Leaping Dolphin*. "Don't be afraid, Max," he imagined her saying as she stroked his face. "I'll be back before you know it..."

Max felt strength surge into his heart. He'd trusted her, just as the Sea Ghosts were trusting him now. *I can't let them down...*

He forced his eyes open and saw he wasn't far from Stinger's brain. The cylinder glowed like before, a few feet away, its shape only just visible through the pink goo. With painful slowness, his fingers drew his blade. Then Max flailed, trying to tear a path through to the tube of swirling light.

But with each clawed handful of slime, the going got tougher. He couldn't breathe air or water. He was so tired, and every limb begged for rest. He let go of the hyperblade. The world became muted, then grey. His chest burned from trying to breathe.

A familiar shape swept past him, nose-sword swiping from side to side through the slime.

Spike!

A hand hooked beneath Max's armpit, and he felt himself heaved free of the goo. Suddenly water poured into his gills, and colour rushed back into his vision. There before him was Lia; her mouth was moving, and Max gradually heard words.

"Max, dead? Bad. Bad."

Rivet?

"…all right?" said Lia. "Max, can you hear me?"

"I'm okay," he mumbled, as his limbs gradually came back to life. Rivet was wagging his tail. "Thank you."

Lia arched her eyebrows. "When will you just listen? I told you— Ouch!"

Max shoved her hard in the chest as a tentacle descended to grab her. Lia's eyes opened wide as she saw it sweep past.

More tendrils were creeping towards them like eager fingers. Rivet dodged out of the way, snapping angrily, and Max jerked to avoid another.

"We're losing," called Lia, swishing back and forth on Spike. "Most of the Sea Ghosts have been taken. The slime's too thick."

Max glanced desperately around. Lia was right. Only a few Sea Ghosts remained and they were holding back. The rest struggled weakly in their slimy coffins. Then, between the dangling stingers, Max spotted his aquabuggy hovering in the water. There was something poking from the seat compartment.

Of course! Shredder's hyperblade!

He'd salvaged the blade from the leg of Shredder the Spider Droid after his last battle. It was three times the size of his hand-held blade. *Just the thing for slicing through Stinger's jelly...*

Almost as if Stinger could sense his plan, a dozen glowing tendrils snaked towards him. Max dived beneath them, and struck out towards the aquabuggy with powerful strokes. As he looked up, he saw that Roger was climbing into its seat. The pirate cast a sneaky look around him, then engaged the engines.

"Hey!" said Max.

Roger glanced back, and even through his helmet, Max saw him blush. His gaze shifted from Max to the shape of Stinger looming above him. He frowned. *He was thinking of stealing my buggy!* Max realised.

"Get over here!" he cried.

Roger looked towards the open sea for a second, then turned the buggy around and zoomed in Max's direction. "I was just coming to rescue you," said Roger, winking his one eye.

"Hmm," said Lia. "It looked more like you were running away."

"And abandon my crew? No chance!" said Roger.

Max didn't have time to argue. "Keep Stinger busy," he said. He snatched the large hyperblade from under the buggy's seat, and kicked towards the gash in Stinger's body he'd already made. Tangled wiring spilled from one end of the blade, where he'd torn it free of Shredder's leg. Stinger pulsed and jerked, trying to throw him off, but Max gripped a handful of slime with one hand, and slashed again and again with the hyperblade. His arm burned, but he didn't give up. At last, with Max's shoulder screaming in pain, the cylinder was exposed.

Now I've got you... thought Max, and he stabbed the blade right into the heart of the glowing tube.

It bounced off harmlessly. Max tried again, and the shock jarred his arm.

Now what? Why hadn't he thought of this? Of course the Professor wasn't going to make it easy to destroy Stinger's brain!

"Max!" Rivet barked. "Pistol!"

His dogbot shot forward. *Yes! Roger's blaster!* Max opened the compartment in Rivet's back and pulled out the gun. But as soon as he had it out, a tendril clasped around Rivet's middle and jerked him through the water. The dogbot yelped as he was dragged away.

Max dived after him, but already he could see several stingers moving towards him. He might be able to dodge one, but not five. They'd shock the life out of him, frying his insides.

Max could hear Rivet's panicked howls as he flailed in the monster's grip. He wanted to save his dogbot, but in a moment the stingers would have him too.

There was only one thing for it. He spun around, aiming the blaster pistol at the

cylinder. As the first of Stinger's tentacles touched his leg, he pulled the trigger.

CHAPTER NINE

A FRESH TRAIL

The blaster jerked in his hand and light blinded him. Max expected to feel the pain of five stings, but he felt nothing at all. As he opened his eyes, he saw a jagged hole in the side of the cylinder, and smoke pouring from it. Several tendrils flopped close to his body, completely lifeless. Flashes lit up across Stinger's body like sheet lightning in storm clouds, and sparks fizzed and crackled along its circuits.

The great jellyfish beast let out a low

moan that seemed to vibrate deep in Max's bones. One by one, the lights across its body dimmed and went out, like the windows of Aquora's skyscrapers at night. Soon the entire shape was dark, and its tendrils hung motionless.

Rivet tugged himself free of the tendril

that had caught him and swam up to Max, panting and grinning.

"Good shot, Max!" called Lia from below.

He turned and saw her waiting beside the aquabuggy with Roger and Spike.

Beneath the vast underbelly of the Professor's creature, Sea Ghosts were pulling free of the slime. They gathered in small groups, marvelling at the monstrous shape of Stinger as it drifted in the current. Rivet snapped at one of the dangling tentacles.

Max stuck the blaster under his belt and swam back towards his friends.

"We did it!" said Roger. "I knew that creature was no match for my crew! I wonder if there's a reward."

"Your crew?" said Lia. "From where I was treading water, it looked like you were planning to ditch us."

Roger puffed out his chest. "That's an insult to my seaman's honour, young lady."

"Stinger is done for now," said Max, handing the blaster back to the pirate. "The Sea Ghosts won't need to be afraid any more." Max knew he'd done the right thing in fighting Stinger. Wasn't that why he was here – to protect this underwater world and stop the Professor from attacking Sumara?

"But what do we do with that?" asked Lia, pointing to Stinger's body. Great globs of slime were drooling from its underside.

"Let it drift," said Max. "It will float away from Spectron soon enough, and when the Professor comes looking for it, he'll get a nasty surprise."

The Sea Ghosts swam up closer to the giant jellyfish, clinging to its body.

"What are they doing?" asked Lia.

Max smiled as he watched the Sea Ghosts go to work tugging the robotic components out. "They're scavenging," he said. "That's what they do, remember? Actually, it's a good idea. One of those stingers might come in useful. Fetch, Rivet!"

The dogbot yapped and sped off to the nearest drooping tendril. With his metal teeth, he tore one of the robotic stingers free and swam back. Max examined it closely. It was about the length of his arm, spongy and slightly sticky, but it felt strong. The stinger glowed a ghostly pink. Max was careful to avoid it as he stowed the tendril together with the spider's-leg hyperblade in the aquabuggy's seat. Then, climbing on board, he steered the buggy back towards the seabed.

"I suppose I should thank you for coming to help," Max said to Roger, who was swimming alongside.

"For not running away, more like," grumbled Lia, swishing past on Spike. "But at least you fought against your pirate instincts."

"How many times do I have to tell you, I'm not a pirate!" said Roger. As he engaged his boot thrusters, a jewelled chain fell from his sleeve. He snatched it up and grinned widely. His golden tooth sparkled.

"Of course you're not," said Lia, and rolled her eyes at Roger.

Suddenly Max felt the hair on the back of his neck stand up. He pulled up the aquabuggy and spun around. Hundreds of Sea Ghosts were hovering in the water. "You shouldn't sneak up on people like that!" he said, smiling.

At the front were Ko and his mother. Already Allis was looking brighter, less hunched, and smiling broadly. "We see fight from healer's boat," Ko said aloud. "All Spectron give you thanks."

Max felt a wave of gratitude crash over him, silent but heartfelt. The green eyes of the Sea Ghosts glowed with joy.

Thank you...

...blessings to your people...

...great courage...

"You all fought bravely," said Max. "The Professor will think twice before attacking your city again." He couldn't help wondering what else his uncle might have in store, but at least Stinger the Sea Phantom had been stopped.

A low rumble made the city vibrate. "It sleeps again," said Allis. "Spectron is safe."

"Exactly what is this creature beneath the city?" asked Lia.

But the group of Sea Ghosts was silent, even inside Max's head. They parted, and the old Ghost who lived in the *Leaping Dolphin* swam forward. He extended a hand to Max. In his other hand, he held the strange robotic conch shell from his mother's vessel.

"I want you to have this," the Sea Ghost said, "as a token of our thanks. It was your mother's, so now it should be yours."

Max thought for a moment about refusing the gift, but he knew he couldn't. This might be the last trace of her that he found below the waves. "Thank you," he said. "This means a lot to me."

He held the shell gingerly in his hand, turning it over to inspect the circuitry. There wasn't even any obvious way to switch it on, but that didn't matter. It was a link to his missing mother, and one day he would discover its purpose.

He looked up and saw that Roger was staring at him, an odd expression on his face.

"What?" asked Max.

"It's nothing." Roger shrugged. "Just... I didn't realise your mother was an undersea explorer as well. You see, I met a human woman who looked a bit like you, about a year back. Me and my crew were—"

"A year!" gasped Max, gripping Roger's shoulders.

"Hey!" said Roger, trying to pull himself

free. "Ease up, whippersnapper!"

"You met my mother a year ago?" said Max in amazement. "But..."

His mind reeled. The Professor had

taunted him with the possibility that his mother might be alive still, but Max hadn't dared to believe it was true. But if Roger had seen her just a year ago, then maybe it was true and she hadn't died after all...

"Tell me!" he said. "Where did you meet her?"

Roger grinned and shrugged. "I can take you to the spot where I met her, if you like. I reckon I owe you."

Max looked at Lia, who smiled, a little uncertainly. *She doesn't know whether to trust him or not*, he thought. But she said, "I'll go with you, of course."

Max dashed to Ko and Allis, and shook them both by the hand. The Sea Ghosts looked startled.

"Sorry, but we have to leave," said Max. "I hope we'll see you again one day."

He jumped onto the aquabuggy, and

steered it to face the open ocean. "Which way?" he said to Roger.

The pirate unclipped a handheld device from his belt. "Well, let me consult my charts."

Max's heart was thumping like a drum. They had beaten the Professor's latest Robobeast, but he knew that it wouldn't be the end of his uncle's plans to destroy the underwater worlds and seize control of the oceans. But now Roger's words sent Max's thoughts in another direction.

He imagined rushing into his mother's arms. He imagined finding her, and taking her home to his father.

Max stared into the vast emptiness of the ocean, and Rivet nuzzled at his side.

If you're out there somewhere, Mum, I'll find you...

In the next Sea Quest adventure, Max must face

CRUSHER
THE CREEPING TERROR

Read on for an exclusive extract...

"You really knew my mother?" Max said.

"Aye," Roger said. "I knew her."

Max sat in his aquabuggy, ready to leave Spectron, the city of the Sea Ghosts, with his pet dogbot Rivet, his Merryn friend Lia and her swordfish, Spike. Together they had just defeated Stinger – the deadly jellyfish Robobeast created by Max's evil uncle, the Professor, to terrorise Spectron. The giant, broken form of Stinger drifted in the current above the undersea city, no longer glowing with light. Its dangling tentacles hung above the wrecked ships that were the Sea Ghosts' homes. But Max wasn't looking at the jellyfish any more, for he was too shocked and surprised. He had just been told that his missing mother had been seen only a year ago.

Max stared at Roger, the man with the eye patch and ponytail they'd met on their travels, who claimed he wasn't a pirate but looked and spoke exactly like one. Roger had just offered to take Max and his friends to the place where he'd met Max's mother. Max couldn't wait to get going, but Roger was busy checking his rocketboots were still in working order.

"So – how did you meet her?" Max asked.

"We travelled together for a while," Roger said.

"I met her in the Crystal Forest, a day's journey to the east, on the other side of the mountains."

Max's heart beat faster. He looked down at the conch shell he held in his hands. It had been modified with some kind of electronics – there were wires and buttons and circuits inside, but he had no idea what they did. It had been made and left here by his mother, the Sea Ghosts had told him. Max had begun this quest to defeat the Professor, and had never expected to find out so much about his long-lost mum. It seemed as if every clue pointed back to her.

"Well, come on then," Max said to Roger. "I'm ready when you are!"

SEA QUEST

Look out for all the books in
Sea Quest Series 3:

THE PRIDE OF BLACKHEART

TETRAX THE SWAMP CROCODILE
NEPHRO THE ICE LOBSTER
FINARIA THE SAVAGE SEA SNAKE
CHAKROL THE OCEAN HAMMER

OUT IN MARCH 2014!

Don't miss the
BRAND NEW
Special Bumper Edition:

STENGOR
THE CRAB MONSTER

978 1 40831 852 2

OUT IN NOVEMBER 2013

WIN AN EXCLUSIVE GOODY BAG

In every Sea Quest book the Sea Quest logo is hidden in one of the pictures. Find the logos in books 5–8, make a note of which pages they appear on and go online to enter the competition at

www.seaquestbooks.co.uk

Each month we will put all of the correct entries into a draw and select one winner to receive a special Sea Quest goody bag.

You can also send your entry on a postcard to:

Sea Quest Competition, Orchard Books,
338 Euston Road, London, NW1 3BH

Don't forget to include your name and address!

GOOD LUCK

Closing Date: December 30th 2013

IF YOU LIKE SEA QUEST, YOU'LL LOVE **BEAST QUEST!**

FREE COLLECTOR CARDS INSIDE!

Series 1: COLLECT THEM ALL!

An evil wizard has enchanted the magical beasts of Avantia. Only a true hero can free the beasts and save the land. Is Tom the hero Avantia has been waiting for?

978 1 84616 483 5

978 1 84616 482 8

978 1 84616 484 2

978 1 84616 486 6

978 1 84616 485 9

978 1 84616 487 3

DON'T MISS THE
BRAND NEW SERIES OF:

Series 14: THE CURSED DRAGON

RAFFKOR
THE STAMPEDING BRUTE

978 1 40832 920 7

VISLAK
THE SLITHERING SERPENT

978 1 40832 921 4

TIKRON
THE JUNGLE MASTER

978 1 40832 922 1

FALRA
THE SNOW PHOENIX

978 1 40832 923 8

OUT IN JANUARY 2014!